THE DRAMATIC LIFE OF AZALEAH LANE

BY NIKKI SHANNON SMITH

ILLUSTRATED BY GLORIA FELIX

PICTURE WINDOW BOOKS
a capstone imprint

Azaleah Lane is published by Picture Window Books,
an imprint of Capstone.
1710 Roe Crest Drive
North Mankato, Minnesota 56003
www.capstonepub.com

Library of Congress Cataloging-in-Publication Data
Names: Smith, Nikki Shannon, 1971– author.
Title: The dramatic life of Azaleah Lane / by Nikki Shannon Smith.
Description: North Mankato, Minnesota : Picture Window Books, an
imprint of Capstone, [2020] | Series: Azaleah Lane | Audience: Ages
6–8. | Summary: Azaleah's older sister, Nia, is going to be the star of the
school musical, but things keep going wrong at the rehearsal: missing
batteries, disappearing props, microphones that suddenly do not work.
Mr. Guidi, the director, blames the ghost of Thespis, but Azaleah suspects
that somebody is actually sabotaging the show. She is determined to use
her detective skills to uncover the culprit and set things right so the play
will be a complete success.
Identifiers: LCCN 2019057095 (print) | LCCN 2019057096 (ebook) | ISBN
9781515844655 (hardcover) | ISBN 9781515844693 (adobe pdf)
Subjects: LCSH: African American girls—Juvenile fiction. | Middle-
born children—Juvenile fiction. | Sisters—Juvenile fiction. | Children's
plays—Juvenile fiction. | Musicals—Juvenile fiction. | Malicious
mischief—Juvenile fiction. | Detective and mystery stories. | CYAC:
Mystery and detective stories. | African Americans—Fiction. | Middle-
born children—Fiction. | Sisters—Fiction. | Theater—Fiction. | GSAFD:
Mystery fiction. | LCGFT: Detective and mystery fiction.
Classification: LCC PZ7.S6566 Dr 2020 (print) | LCC PZ7.S6566 (ebook)
| DDC 813.6 [Fic]—dc23
LC record available at https://lccn.loc.gov/2019057095
LC ebook record available at https://lccn.loc.gov/2019057096

Image Credits: Shutterstock: Beskova Ekaterina, design element
throughout

Designer: Kay Fraser

Printed in the United States of America.
003354

TABLE OF CONTENTS

HEY, THERE! I'M AZALEAH!

I'm eight years old and in the third grade. My life is *amazing*. I live in Washington, D.C., with my family: Mama, Daddy, Nia, and Tiana. Washington, D.C., is our nation's capital and the *coolest* place to grow up.

Mama has her very own restaurant here called Avec Amour. That means "with love" in French. She named it that because she adds love to everything she does.

My daddy is a lawyer. He sues bad guys for a living. The bad guys are big businesses that do things that hurt other people. But my daddy makes them pay. He makes sure they're held responsible.

Tiana is my baby sister. She's four years old and pretty cute—most of the time. I like her a lot, even though she comes in my room too much. I also have an older sister named Nia. She's in middle school and is always in her room. *Always.*

Mama's sister—my Auntie Sam—takes care of us when Mama and Daddy are busy. I love Auntie Sam. She's never too tired to play and she likes to do art. She also likes adventures—my favorite!

Aside from my family, there are three main things you should know about me.

1. I'm curious . . . *not* nosy. (Despite what Nia says.)

2. I'm good at solving mysteries—very good.

3. I live in the White House!

OK . . . not the *real* White House. (The president of the United States lives there.) But my house is big and white, plus it has a great big living room and a nice backyard. It's just as good as the real White House, if you ask me!

IT'S HARD TO BELIEVE THIS AMAZING LIFE ALL BELONGS TO ME, AZALEAH LANE!

CHAPTER 1

WILLA WONKA AND HER SISTER

"Action!" the drama teacher yelled.

The theater lights dimmed. Actors came onto the stage. I couldn't believe my luck. I was about to watch a top-secret rehearsal at my big sister's middle school!

I stared up at the stage. A beautiful candy garden had been set up there. My older sister, Nia, was up there too. She wore a long, glittery purple coat and a matching purple top hat. The dark theater and bright spotlight made the coat look even shinier.

Nia had been talking about her costume for weeks. She was the lead in her school's next show, *Willa Wonka and the Chocolate Factory.*

Willy Wonka was originally supposed to be a boy. But Nia's teacher, Mr. Guidi, had changed the name to *Willa* Wonka just for her.

Now I could finally see why my sister kept saying her costume was awesome. It was gorgeous!

I watched while Nia sang a song about imagination. The other actors stood nearby, amazed by the garden around them. They were the visitors at the chocolate factory.

I leaned forward. Nia sang in a soft, dreamy voice. She sounded even better than she did when she practiced at home.

Suddenly, Mr. Guidi, yelled, "Cut!"

Everyone froze—including my sister. She looked very upset.

I don't think Nia wants to stop, I thought.

A boy came out from the back.

"What happened to the lights, Mike?" Mr. Guidi asked. "Why is the coat not lighting up?"

What is he talking about? I wondered.

Mike held up a remote control. "The batteries are gone!"

"They were there yesterday," said Nia.

At the end of my row, a boy with long, curly hair giggled. I didn't think it was very funny. I wanted to tell him to stop laughing, but I couldn't. I had promised Mama I'd be quiet.

I wasn't even supposed to be at the rehearsal. Mama usually took me, Nia, and our little sister, Tiana, to her restaurant after school on Friday afternoons. We'd stay at Avec Amour until Daddy or Auntie Sam picked us up.

Auntie Sam watched us all the time. Between Mama's restaurant and Daddy's job as a lawyer, my parents were pretty busy. I loved being with Auntie Sam. We always had fun.

But today after school had been very unusual. When I got to Mama's car, my little sister wasn't there.

"Where's Tiana?" I asked.

"She's at her friend Kevin's house playing," Mama said. "It's the mayor's birthday today, and she's celebrating with dinner at Avec Amour. That means I can't bring you to work with me today."

"Why?" I asked.

"The mayor's party is in the private dining room," Mama explained. "You can't be in there, and you can't sit alone for three hours. Daddy is working late, and Auntie Sam is out of town."

There was nobody to watch me. That's how I ended up at Nia's rehearsal. Mr. Guidi had agreed I could stay there for the evening. But he had what Mama called *conditions*.

1. I had to stay seated.
2. I had to stay quiet.

Mama had reminded me about this three times before she left. That's why I couldn't tell the boy to stop laughing.

I wonder why he's allowed to be in the theater, I thought. *Does he have conditions too?*

Mr. Guidi crossed his arms and looked at everyone. "Batteries!" he yelled.

Every light in the theater came on. All the kids onstage looked nervous. Nia looked like she was about to cry. She took her shows very seriously.

Nia was what Daddy called a "triple threat." That meant she could dance, sing, *and* act. She was always in a show. She had been the main character before. But this was the first time Mr. Guidi had changed a character just for her.

It was a really big deal. Our family was even planning a special surprise party for Nia. It would be at Avec Amour on Sunday after the show. I was in charge of making decorations.

But the party wouldn't be any fun if Nia was sad about the show. Onstage, everyone was standing in silence.

Then I had an idea. I'd noticed a TV in the lobby when I got to the theater. I had a feeling it had a remote with batteries.

I knew I was supposed to stay seated and quiet. I really wanted to help, though. Nia needed me.

I had two choices.

1. I could follow the conditions.
2. I could interrupt.

My heart started to beat fast. I knew I might get in trouble with Mr. Guidi. I knew Mama and Daddy would find out I hadn't listened. I also knew Nia might get mad at me.

But I did it anyway.

"Mr. Guidi!" I stood up and yelled. "I have an idea!"

THE GHOST OF THESPIS

Everyone in the whole entire theater stared at me. The laughing boy in my row frowned. A few rows back, an older boy gave me a curious glance.

From the stage, Nia glared at me. It looked like she was trying to shoot laser beams out of her eyes.

Mr. Guidi didn't look happy either. He said, "Azaleah, your mother promised me you would behave if I let you stay here this afternoon."

Just then, one of the fake lollipops in the candy garden fell over. It made all the other lollipops fall like dominoes.

Mr. Guidi rubbed his hands over his face. "Falling props, missing batteries, interrupting children . . . what's next?"

Suddenly a door somewhere in the theater slammed. We all jumped.

"Too many things are going wrong," said Mr. Guidi. "It's the ghost of Thespis." He shook his head and walked toward me.

The closer Mr. Guidi got, the more I worried. Maybe I should have just stayed quiet.

"Well, what is it?" Mr. Guidi frowned at me.

The boy I'd seen laughing about the coat covered his mouth and laughed at me.

I wish Mr. Guidi would turn around and catch him, I thought.

I focused on Mr. Guidi. "There's a TV in the lobby," I told him. "You know the one that shows the stage? I saw it on my way in. Does it have a remote? Maybe we could use the batteries from there."

Mr. Guidi's whole face changed. He smiled at me and turned to the laughing boy. The boy stopped laughing just in time.

"Owen," Mr. Guidi said, "go get the batteries from the lobby TV remote!"

Owen popped up and ran toward the lobby.

I grinned, and my heart slowed down. It was a good thing I was so observant. Observant people noticed things other people didn't.

I was also a good listener. I hadn't forgotten what Mr. Guidi said.

"What is the ghost of Thespis?" I asked.

"*Who* is the ghost of Thespis," Mr. Guidi corrected me. "Thespis was the first actor ever. If things go wrong in the theater, it's usually him."

I couldn't tell if Mr. Guidi was serious or not. A few of the kids were nodding like they believed him. In the audience, the older boy I'd noticed was writing something down.

Before I could ask any questions, Owen came back with the batteries. He gave them to Mike. Mike popped them into the remote. I held my breath as he pressed a button.

The coat lit up, and I let out my breath. The coat was even more amazing with the lights on.

Mr. Guidi turned back to me and clapped. "You're a genius! We need someone like you around here. You're welcome to come back tomorrow."

I grinned and sat back down in my seat, right in the middle of the row. Owen frowned and went back to his seat.

The lights went out. "Take it from the top of the scene," Mr. Guidi said.

Nia had to start her song all over again. This time her coat lit up while she was singing. As Nia's voice got louder, the lights inside the purple coat got brighter and brighter. It almost looked like the coat was glowing.

I stood up and clapped when Nia finished. She had done an excellent job. Owen didn't laugh this time. This time, there was nothing to laugh at.

* * *

For a while, things went fine. But then, during the Oompa Loompa song, everything started going wrong.

First, something happened with the microphones the actors had on their shirts. One microphone turned off. Then another. And then another.

The song got quieter and quieter. Soon all seven microphones were off. The Oompa

Loompas were dancing and singing, but I could barely hear them.

Mr. Guidi yelled, "Cut!"

Mike ran out from backstage. "I'll go check the connection," he said. Then he disappeared.

At the end of our row, Owen giggled—again. It was like he *wanted* the show to be bad.

Onstage, Nia crossed her arms. I watched her chest go up and down. I could tell she was taking deep breaths.

When Mike came back out, he looked confused. "The cord fell out of the plug somehow. It should be fine now."

The rehearsal started again. But a few minutes later, the wooden petals fell off one of the fake flowers in the garden.

The petals made loud *bangs!* when they landed on the ground. The Oompa Loompas kept tripping over petals and kicking them. They were sliding all over the stage. Nia had

to keep looking down so she didn't step on the kids or the petals.

"Keep going!" yelled Mr. Guidi. "We don't have time to fix them right now."

If there really is a ghost of Thespis, he sure is busy, I thought.

Owen laughed again, but this time Mr. Guidi heard him.

"That's enough, Owen," he snapped.

Owen stopped laughing right away. I smiled. I was glad Mr. Guidi had finally caught him.

The crew picked up the petals, but then the string that opened and closed the curtains broke. Mr. Guidi had to stop everything so the crew could tie the ends together.

A few minues later, the bubble machine that was supposed to blow bubbles on the stage ran out of bubble soap. They had to

stop to refill it. When they started again,
Nia messed up her lines.

The rehearsal wasn't going well at all.
The only good thing was that Owen wasn't
laughing anymore.

Every time something went wrong, I thought
about the ghost of Thespis. I didn't think a
ghost could ruin a whole rehearsal. But it
seemed like a lot of bad luck for one show.
Something strange was going on.

Finally, the rehearsal was over. Mr. Guidi said loudly, "Everyone, gather around, please."

He motioned to the teenager I'd seen sitting a few rows back. The boy came forward and joined the cast. He had a tiny recorder in one hand and a notebook in the other.

"This is Chris," said Mr. Guidi. "He's a reporter for the high school newspaper. He's hoping to write a good story about the musical."

Nia's eyes got big. Some of the actors smiled at Chris.

A reporter? I thought. *No wonder he seemed like he was paying attention to everything.*

Mr. Guidi kept talking. "I've given him a backstage tour and time to explore. He has full permission to be anywhere in the theater. Chris will be at the dress rehearsal tomorrow and the show on Sunday."

I knew all about dress rehearsals because Nia had been in so many shows. It was the last chance to get things right. It was supposed to be as good as the real show, even though there was no audience.

At dress rehearsals, all the actors wore their costumes and stage makeup. They didn't stop to fix things, even if something went wrong. Nia always said, "The show must go on."

Mr. Guidi looked at all the actors. "We have a lot of work to do if we want a flawless production and a good review," he said.

I knew what *flawless* meant. It meant perfect. And one thing was for sure: this show was *not* perfect.

CHAPTER 3

FOUL PLAY

When we got to the lobby, Daddy was waiting for us. "How did it go?" he asked.

Nia burst into tears. "It was a total disaster!"

Daddy looked at me. "What happened?" he asked.

"The rehearsal had . . . a few problems," I said.

"We have to go pick up Tiana. Let's talk about this in the car," said Daddy. Once we were all in the car, he turned to Nia. "So, what happened?"

"My costume didn't light up because the batteries in the remote were missing. Microphones went dead. Props were messed up. Everything went wrong. I messed up my lines," said Nia.

"I'm sure it wasn't that bad," Daddy said.

"It *was* that bad," Nia insisted. "*And* a reporter was there. He's going to write an article for the high school newspaper. If the show is bad, the review will be bad. People are going to think I did a bad job!"

Daddy sighed. "I'm sorry, Nia. I'm sure tomorrow will be better."

"I get to go back tomorrow," I told Daddy. "Mr. Guidi said he needs someone like me around."

"Are you sure that's OK with Mr. Guidi?" Daddy asked.

I nodded.

"Azaleah *was* helpful today," Nia said.

"That's great!" Daddy grinned at me.

The car was very quiet until we got to Kevin's house to pick up Tiana. I was glad to see my little sister. She was usually cheerful.

"Guess what?" Tiana said. She bounced in her booster seat as Daddy buckled her in. "Me and Kevin made ice cream sundaes for snack!"

"Kevin and *I*!" Daddy said, but he was smiling.

Nia stared out of the window while Tiana told us every single detail about her playdate with Kevin. Tiana smiled so much that it made me smile too.

Daddy kept saying, "That sounds like fun."

Finally we got to our house—the White House. It isn't the *real* White House. The president lives there. But I call our house the White House because it's huge and white and beautiful with a big backyard.

I was happy to be home. Plus, it reminded me that I needed to work on the decorations for Nia's party. I would have to start right after dinner. It was already Friday, and now I would be at the rehearsal tomorrow. I wanted to take my time so I would have a beautiful sign by Sunday.

In the kitchen, Daddy took out leftovers from Avec Amour.

"Yummmm!" yelled Tiana. "Crab jambalaya!"

We loved leftovers from Mama's restaurant. They were always a good surprise. We set the table and sat down. Nia still looked sad.

"Daddy, have you ever heard of the ghost of Thespis?" I asked.

Daddy shook his head.

"Mr. Guidi said it's the ghost of the first actor ever," I explained. "When something

goes wrong in the theater, the ghost probably did it."

Tiana gasped. "*A ghost?* That's scary."

"He was just saying that," said Nia. She shook her head at me.

"Are you sure it wasn't just a coincidence?" Daddy asked.

Daddy used the word *coincidence* a lot. He's a lawyer. That means he always has to prove that something is not just a coincidence.

"Well," I said, "it was *a lot* of bad luck. Something strange was *definitely* going on."

Nia stared at me and leaned forward. "Do you think it was foul play?"

"What's foul play?" Tiana and I asked at the same time.

Daddy chuckled. "That means someone is up to no good," he said.

I wasn't sure if it was foul play or not—*yet*.

"Nia, why would someone sabotage your rehearsal?" asked Daddy.

"I don't know," Nia said.

"You shouldn't make assumptions without proof," Daddy said. "You know that, Nia."

Nia didn't answer. Daddy finished his dinner and took Tiana upstairs for her bath. But even though Daddy had left the room, his words didn't leave my brain.

Was it a coincidence? I wondered. *Or is Nia right?*

Since we were alone, I asked Daddy's question again. "Nia, why *would* someone try to ruin rehearsal?"

Nia thought for a while. "All I know is batteries don't just disappear. And that bubble machine was full yesterday."

"Were there problems before today?" I asked.

"Rehearsals always have problems," Nia explained. "We've been practicing for more than two weeks. But none of the rehearsals were *this* bad. The show has gotten worse instead of better."

I still didn't see why anyone would want to mess up Nia's musical. But then I remembered Owen and all of his laughing.

I frowned. "Nia, who is Owen?" I asked.

Before Nia could answer, Daddy came back downstairs. "Nia, can you help me with Tiana?" he asked. "She's ready to get in the tub, but I just remembered I need to call my client before it gets too late."

"OK," Nia said. She picked up her plate and put it in the dishwasher. On her way past, she whispered, "I'll tell you about Owen later."

I cleaned up my plate too. Then I followed Nia up the stairs. She went into the bathroom, and I went to my room.

I had planned to work on the decorations for Nia's surprise party, but now I had a bigger job. I had a mystery to investigate.

I packed some things in my backpack to take to tomorrow's rehearsal:

- binoculars (so I could see the stage—and suspects)
- a sewing kit (in case of more costume problems)
- a notebook and a pencil (so I could write down anything suspicious)
- batteries from my circuit kit (in case there were more disappearing batteries)

Then I ran downstairs and got one more thing: three of Mama's delicious chocolate chip cookies. I put them in a baggie so I'd have a snack tomorrow.

Now I was ready for rehearsal. I loved a challenge, and I was good at solving mysteries. I was not going to let *anyone*— ghost or person—ruin *Willa Wonka*.

UNDERSTUDY (NOT A BUDDY)

I woke up bright and early the next morning and went downstairs. Daddy was already at the kitchen table in his robe working on his laptop. Mama was making waffles.

"Good morning," said Mama. She gave me a kiss on my forehead.

"Hi, Mama," I said. "Why are you up so early? It's Lazy Saturday."

Mama worked late on Friday nights, so she usually slept in on Saturdays. Daddy and I were the early birds. We always ate cereal and watched cartoons together.

Mama smiled. "I took tomorrow off so I can see Nia's show. I have to work early today so I can prep the food."

"Is Nia up yet?" I asked.

Daddy shook his head. "I don't think so."

Just then, Nia walked in. Most of the time, my big sister pretended to be a character in a play, even when she was at home. But today she just looked sad.

Mama looked worried. "Do you feel OK?"

Nia sat at the table with Daddy. "Yeah," she said. "I'm just dreading rehearsal today."

Mama looked even *more* worried. "Why?" she asked. "What's wrong?"

"Yesterday's rehearsal was the worst," Nia said. She gave Mama all the details.

"Well, I'm sure things will be better today," Mama said.

"I doubt it," said Nia. "Especially if someone is doing this on purpose."

"Who would do that?" Mama looked shocked.

I had been waiting to ask Nia the same exact thing. So far, my only suspect was the ghost of Thespis. And I was pretty sure it wasn't him.

"I think it could be Mike or Andrea . . . or Owen." Nia frowned.

Daddy looked up from his laptop. "Nia, what did I say yesterday? Let's not jump to conclusions," he said. "It could be a coincidence."

I did *not* think this was a coincidence. It didn't make sense for the show to get worse. But Daddy was right. We shouldn't blame anyone yet. Not until I investigated.

I knew Mike was the guy with the remote. I'd seen him at rehearsal yesterday.

"Who is Andrea?" I asked.

"She's on the stage crew with Mike. She makes a lot of the props. She thinks it's funny to play jokes on people," said Nia.

If it was Andrea, her jokes were definitely not funny.

"What about Mike?" I asked. "Why would he take the batteries out of his own remote?"

"Because!" Nia was getting upset again. "He's Owen's best friend."

"But why is Owen even *there*?" I asked. I just didn't understand.

Nia let out a huge puff of air. "Owen is the understudy," she said. "He gets to play Willy Wonka if I get sick or something."

"So he wants your part in the show?" I asked.

Nia nodded. "Owen thinks a boy should play Willy Wonka," she said. "And that boy should be *him*. If he and Mike make me mess up, Mr. Guidi will think I'm not practicing. He might give Owen my part."

That was very interesting information. "What will Owen be if he doesn't get your part?" I asked.

"Nothing," said Nia. "Right now he just sits there and watches."

And laughs, I thought. Maybe Owen *had* played tricks during the rehearsal to make Nia mess up. Maybe Mike had helped him.

I knew I had to tell Nia about what I'd seen.

"Owen was sitting by me during rehearsal," I said. "I saw him laughing."

Nia's eyes got big. "You did?"

I nodded. "He laughed *a lot.*"

"That's it. It must be Owen," said Nia. "It has to be."

Mama said, "Maybe you should talk to Mr. Guidi."

"No," said Daddy. "You can't accuse anyone unless you're sure. You need to prove it."

It's a good thing I'm going to the rehearsal today, I thought. *I have a lot of evidence to collect.*

If Owen was the culprit, I would tell Mr. Guidi. I couldn't let Owen ruin the whole show and embarrass my sister.

Since we had time before the dress rehearsal, I went up to my room. I wanted to make a Congratulations sign for Nia's party. I decided I would draw flowers and candy around the border. They would look just like the ones on the stage.

The party was going to be fantastic. Mama and I had planned it together. We had to keep it a secret from Nia *and* Tiana. Tiana was horrible at keeping secrets.

Mama had even planned a special menu of sweet treats. Nia's show was about a candy factory, after all. Auntie Sam was coming too. I couldn't wait!

It took me a whole hour to finish my sign. It looked really good. But the whole time I worked, my mind was on something else—my investigation.

I put my sign away and opened my backpack. I took out my notebook and pencil. I made a list of all of the problems from yesterday. They were the clues.

1. remote batteries missing

2. lollipops fell over

3. microphones stopped working

4. flower petals fell off

5. curtain strings broke

6. bubble machine was empty

Somebody had been *very* busy causing problems yesterday. But now somebody would be looking for that person, and that somebody was *me*.

CHAPTER 5

SNEAKY DETECTIVE

A few hours later, Nia came downstairs. She looked completely different. Her hair was in five big cornrows, so it would fit under the Willa Wonka hat. She had on eye makeup and lipstick too. The only thing missing was her costume.

"Ooooooo! You look so pretty," Tiana said.

Nia smiled and bowed. "Thank you."

"My triple threat!" Daddy clapped for Nia.

"Where's your costume?" Tiana asked.

"It's in the dressing room at the theater," Nia explained. "Mr. Guidi doesn't let us bring them home. He says they're safer backstage."

Daddy, Nia, Tiana, and I got into the car. He was taking us to rehearsal today because Mama needed to be at the restaurant. Saturday nights were busy, plus she was taking tomorrow off for Nia's show.

When we got to the theater, Tiana said, "Azaleah gets to stay? I want to stay too."

"No," said Daddy. "You and I are going to the park."

Tiana cheered. The park was her favorite place.

I followed Nia inside. Owen was in the front row. Chris, the reporter, was sitting a few rows back, talking to Mr. Guidi.

"Can you tell me more about the ghost of Thespis?" I heard him ask. "It might help with my story."

I smiled. Chris was curious, just like me.

"Come backstage with me," Nia whispered. "Maybe you can get an inside look at what's going on back there."

That was the perfect place for me. I would be able to see it all: backstage, onstage, and the audience.

"Am I allowed back there?" I asked. I didn't want to get into trouble.

Nia smiled and took my hand. "Mr. Guidi let Chris look around back there yesterday. It'll be OK." Then she said, "I'm glad you're here."

Nia led me to the stage. A girl dressed in black walked onto the stage and checked all the props.

"Who is that?" I asked Nia.

"That's Andrea," Nia whispered.

Even though Nia had said Andrea liked to play jokes on people, she looked very serious.

I watched her check every single thing on the stage.

"I have to go get changed," Nia said. "Are you OK here?"

I nodded, and Nia rushed off to the dressing room. I hid in a corner behind one of the curtains. I could see everything, and I was out of the way. I put my backpack with my detective equipment on the floor next to me.

Pretty soon, the cast came onto the stage. Nia looked really good in her purple coat and top hat. She carried a walking stick that was also part of her costume.

I peeked around the curtain. Mr. Guidi stood on the floor in front of the stage. Chris, the reporter, stood there with him. Mr. Guidi clapped his hands, and everyone looked at him.

"Chris has asked to interview the lead characters after the show tomorrow," he said.

"We'll have a photographer from the paper here too. Let's make this our best show yet. We want to give Chris something to write about."

Nia glanced at me. She looked worried. Mr. Guidi looked a little worried too. He kept rubbing his hands together like he was putting on invisible lotion.

Chris watched Mr. Guidi for a second. Then he wrote something down in his notebook.

I need to solve this mystery as fast as I can, I thought. We wanted to give Chris something good to write about.

The lights went out and the rehearsal started. I took out my binoculars. I wanted to see each person's face clearly. Andrea pulled the curtains open and the music started.

The dress rehearsal was really good—at first. It was just like watching a real show.

In the beginning, the characters were trying to find golden tickets. The tickets were hidden in chocolate bars at the candy store. A boy named Charlie found one, so he got to go on a special visit to Willa Wonka's Chocolate Factory.

In the next part, Charlie and the other kids who'd found tickets all went to the factory. They were super-excited to meet Willa Wonka. That's when Nia came onstage. Willa Wonka led them into the candy factory.

But when Nia's imagination song started, the lights on her coat went crazy. First they were on, and then they were off. Then they went out of control and started blinking.

I spied through my binoculars. Across the stage, Andrea was peeking out from behind the curtain. She had a big frown on her face.

Next, I spied on Mike. He was standing near the curtain strings. He shook the remote and tapped it against his hand. It looked like he was trying to make the lights work right.

Finally I pointed my binoculars at the audience. Owen was laughing.

I wished Mr. Guidi could stop the rehearsal. I wished he would at least turn around and catch Owen laughing at my sister. But Mr. Guidi was focused on the stage.

Nia's eyes looked upset, but she was a professional. She kept right on singing like nothing was wrong.

Pretty soon it was intermission. Tomorrow, during the real show, that would be when the audience got a break. Mr. Guidi, Chris, and the people on the crew clapped. Owen did not.

Nia smiled, even though I knew she wasn't very happy. Mr. Guidi climbed up onto the stage and stood next to her. Mike came out and joined them.

"Mike, what's wrong with the remote now?" asked Mr. Guidi.

Mike shrugged. "I don't know. The batteries are new. We just replaced them yesterday. Maybe it's the coat."

Mr. Guidi yelled, "Benjamin!"

A boy ran out carrying an Oompa Loompa costume. "Yes, Mr. Guidi?"

"You're in charge of wardrobe. What's going on with this coat?"

Benjamin looked embarrassed. "I don't know, Mr. Guidi. I tested it after yesterday's rehearsal. It was fine."

Mr. Guidi let out a gigantic sigh. "The show is tomorrow. There's no time to buy a new coat. We'll have to use it with no effects."

"But Mr. Guidi," said Benjamin, "the special effects are important. Nia is singing about imagination. The coat lights make the song feel magical."

Mr. Guidi hung his head. "We don't have a choice. The show must go on."

CHAPTER 6

INTERMISSION

Nia started to cry. Andrea ran over to her. "It's OK, Nia," she said. "Nobody will even know the coat is supposed to light up."

Mike patted Nia's back. "I'm really sorry. Your singing is so beautiful you don't even need the lights," he said.

I took out my notebook and wrote: *Mike and Andrea were nice to Nia. Probably not the culprits.*

Then I added: *Unless they are faking it. Also, Owen did not clap.*

Andrea walked away to close the curtains. Everyone left the stage to get ready for the next scene. Only Nia stood in the middle of the stage. She took off her hat and hung her head.

I stared at my sister and tried to figure out how to help. Finally, I got an idea. We needed to have what Daddy called a sidebar. Lawyers and judges had those in court when they wanted to talk privately.

I went over to Nia and took her hand. Then I walked her back to my hiding spot. She sat with me and put her face in her hands. She cried and cried.

"Nia," I said. "It's going to be OK. You did a really good job. Did you see the cast clapping for you?"

Nia looked up. "They clapped?"

"You didn't notice?" I asked.

"No," said Nia. "I was too upset."

"People really liked your performance." I smiled at her. "They seemed impressed by

the way you kept going. I was really proud
of you."

Nia smiled—a real smile this time. "Thanks,
Azaleah. You're a good sister." She stood up
and looked down at me. "I'm going to go take
a break before intermission is over."

"Break a leg," I said.

In the theater, it was bad luck to say, "Good
luck." You had to say "Break a leg" instead.

I watched Nia hurry away. I was the
only one left on the stage now. The curtains

were closed. It was the perfect time for an investigation.

I crept over and studied the lollipops. I wanted to see how they were made. Then maybe I could figure out why they had fallen. I noticed that each lollipop stick screwed into a big wooden stand at the bottom.

I thought back to yesterday. The stand hadn't fallen over with the lollipops. The lollipops must not have been screwed in tight.

Just then the theater lights flickered. That meant the show was about to start again.

I hurried to the flowers to inspect the petals. If the petals were glued on, maybe they'd just fallen off.

But when I checked the flowers, I couldn't believe my eyes. The petals were attached with screws. There was only one way they could have come off.

Someone must have unscrewed them, I thought.

The actors hadn't come back yet, so I ran to inspect the curtain strings. I was looking at the knot somebody had tied to fix the problem when I heard a voice behind me.

"What are you doing?"

I turned around. It was Andrea.

"I was looking at this knot," I said. "Do these strings usually break?"

Andrea leaned close to me. "They never break," she said. "Look how thick they are." She had a very angry look on her face.

Andrea was right. The strings were more like rope. It didn't seem like they would just break.

"I think someone did this on purpose," she added.

I was convinced. This was no coincidence. This *was* foul play. And Andrea was furious about it. She was definitely not the one ruining the show. There was no way she'd mess up her own props.

Before I could say anything else, the actors came back out to the stage. I decided to sit in the audience for the rest of the rehearsal. Maybe I would notice something different from there.

I sat down and took out my cookies. I had worked up an appetite with all my investigating.

For the rest of the dress rehearsal, Nia did the best she could. But her magical purple coat wasn't magical anymore, and her voice was sad.

When the rehearsal ended, I glanced back at where Chris sat. His head was down, and he was writing very, very fast.

I had a bad feeling that whatever he was writing wasn't good.

CHAPTER 7

THE DRESSING ROOM

Watching Chris write in his notebook reminded me I needed to add to my notes too. When everyone had left the stage, I took out my notebook and wrote:

- Flower petals and lollipops unscrewed?
- Curtain strings too thick to break. (Andrea did not do it.)

I was positive someone was up to no good. And that meant the lights going out on Nia's purple coat wasn't a coincidence either. I needed to investigate that coat.

I climbed onstage and slipped behind a curtain, like I had seen Nia do earlier. There was an open door back there, which led to a hallway. I followed the sound of voices and found the dressing room.

Nia was inside, putting her hat in a box. A lot of the actors were already gone, but Owen, Mike, and Chris were still there. The three of them were talking in a corner of the room. I wondered if Chris was interviewing them.

"Nia, can I see your coat?" I asked.

Nia handed it to me. "What for? Like Mr. Guidi said, there's no time to fix it." She went behind a screen in the corner to change out of her costume.

First, I examined the outside of the coat. It looked fine. I touched the fabric. I could feel wires and little light bulbs inside.

Next, I turned the coat inside out. It was lined with silky, purple cloth. I couldn't see

the light bulbs or wires that way either. They were in between the layers.

Then I noticed something strange—a few tiny rips in the cloth. That was *very* strange. Nia took good care of her things, especially costumes.

I carefully hung up the coat before Nia could see it. I hadn't told Nia about my investigation yet. I decided it would be better not to. She would just get more upset if she knew about the curtain string and props. If I told her about the rips in her coat, she'd cry even more.

I took out my notebook and wrote: *Tiny rips in coat.*

I was putting my notebook away when Chris walked up to me. "Hi, I'm Chris," he said. "Are you part of the show?"

I shook my head. "I'm Azaleah," I said. "Nia's sister."

Chris's eyes got big. "Oh, wow," he said. "Your sister is really talented. It's too bad the ghost of Thespis showed up."

"You believe in the ghost of Thespis?" I asked.

"Definitely," said Chris. "If it weren't for him, this show would be amazing."

I didn't tell Chris what I thought was going on. I didn't want him to put it in his story. I wanted his story to be good.

"I think the show is amazing anyway," I said.

Chris nodded. "It's a good show. Don't worry, I'll explain that the problems weren't because of the actors. I know it was the ghost of Thespis. I'll make sure my readers know that too."

I wanted to say something good about my sister. Maybe Chris would put it in the story.

"Well . . .," I finally said. "Nia did a great job even though the lights on her coat were messed up."

"Yes, she did," Chris agreed. "I was just talking to Owen. He said he's glad he didn't get the lead. He wouldn't want to be in Nia's shoes. This ghost is ruining everything."

Owen is glad he didn't get the part? I thought.

I didn't know what to think about that. If Owen didn't want the part anymore, maybe that meant he wasn't a suspect. And if Owen wasn't a suspect, that would mean Mike wasn't either.

But maybe Owen was just saying that so nobody would suspect him.

Just then, Nia joined us. "Azaleah, we better go," she said.

I nodded. I was glad Nia hadn't heard Chris. If she knew his article was going to be about a ghost wrecking the show, she'd be upset. I decided to keep it to myself.

When we got in the car, Daddy asked, "Well, was today better?"

I nodded. "Yes." It was true. The dress rehearsal had been perfect except for the coat.

Nia disagreed. "It wasn't better!" she exclaimed. "My coat is broken. The lights were turning on and off and flashing. It was horrible."

"I'm sorry, Nia," said Daddy.

I could tell he felt really bad for her. He didn't ask about foul play, and I knew why. Daddy didn't want any extra drama.

"This musical is going to be a disaster!" wailed Nia. "Everything is ruined. Chris is going to write a bad review."

Nia was having what Mama called a *meltdown*. Tiana had them all the time when she needed a nap.

"The coat is a pretty big deal," I said. "But at least there were no other problems. And Nia was really good."

Nia sniffled and looked out of the window.

At home, Daddy put on one of his old records. He had hundreds of them. He put on one of Nia's favorites: Chaka Khan. I knew he was trying to cheer her up.

"I have an idea," said Daddy. He disappeared into the kitchen. When he came back, he had four bowls in one hand and two boxes of cereal under his arms. He carried a gallon of milk in his other hand.

"Cereal?" I asked.

Tiana cracked up. "Daddy's silly! Cereal is for breakfast."

"Not always," said Daddy. "Haven't you ever heard of *brinner*?"

Nia, Tiana, and I shook our heads.

"Brinner is breakfast for dinner." Daddy looked proud of himself. He started dancing to the music.

Nia smiled. "Whatever, Dad."

We listened to music while we ate brinner. Nia even smiled a little bit. But when it was time for bed, she started to look sad again. I knew she was thinking about the show and her coat.

I wished I knew how to help my sister. This mystery had gotten more and more complicated. I had a bunch of evidence and no suspects. And I was almost out of time. The show was tomorrow.

Tomorrow is not going to be a good day, I thought. *Unless I solve this mystery.*

CHAPTER 8

WHAT IF . . .?

While I got ready for bed, I thought about the mystery. I needed to start at the beginning: Friday, at rehearsal.

The batteries had gone missing, but when Mike put new ones in, the coat worked just fine. That meant it wasn't the remote. It was definitely the coat.

I thought about the inside of the coat. There were lights in between the fabric. I had definitely felt the wires connecting them.

I looked up at the string of lights in my room. The coat lights were probably just like them, but very tiny.

But what's wrong with them? I wondered as I stared at my lights. *What do those tiny rips have to do with it?*

I took my notebook out of my backpack and read my notes again. I didn't think Andrea or Mike had anything to do with this. They were trying hard to make sure things worked.

I put my notebook away and decided to play with my circuit kit. I needed a break from this mystery. I took the batteries out of my backpack. If the remote wasn't the problem, I wouldn't need them anyway.

I put the batteries back in the circuit kit. But the little green light bulb didn't come on like it was supposed to.

I took the batteries out and put them in again. I made sure they were each facing the right direction. Daddy had showed me the + and - on the batteries, so I knew how. But the light still didn't come on.

I wiggled the wires. That didn't help either. The only thing left was the bulb.

I checked the bulb. It wobbled when I touched it. It was very loose, so I tightened it. The light glowed right away.

I turned off my bedroom light and climbed into bed. The glow from the circuit kit made my whole room look green.

I relaxed and closed my eyes. I needed to get some sleep so I'd be ready for tomorrow.

It was almost showtime.

* * *

The next morning, Nia had to be at the theater early. The cast needed to warm up for the show and make sure everything was ready. This was my last chance to figure things out.

Daddy dropped Nia and me off in front of the theater. "See you in a little while," he said. "I can't wait to see the show!"

"Thanks, Dad," said Nia quietly.

My big sister was stressed out, and I didn't blame her. I was *not* doing a good enough job solving this mystery. I just couldn't figure out who was behind all the problems. Plus, I had no idea how or *why* they were doing it.

Owen was still the main suspect. But there was also evidence that he was innocent. He had told Chris he didn't even want to be Willy Wonka.

As I followed Nia inside, I kept thinking about the rips inside the coat. They were too strange.

When we got to the dressing room, I decided to take one more look at Nia's coat. I was running out of time. But before I could inspect it, Mr. Guidi interrupted me.

"Azaleah," he said, "you'll have to wait in the audience today. No guests backstage on show day."

"OK, Mr. Guidi," I said.

I had failed. This mystery was just too hard. I went and sat in the front row by myself. I waited for my family and thought about Nia's coat. There had to be *something* I wasn't getting.

I sat by myself for a little while. I really wished I could be with my sister. Then the seats in the audience started to fill up. Mama, Daddy, Auntie Sam, and Tiana finally came and sat with me.

Auntie Sam gave me a kiss. "Is Nia ready for the show?" she asked.

"I guess so," I said. I knew Nia would do her best even if her coat was broken.

I noticed a photographer taking pictures of the audience. Chris was at the end of the front row, taking notes.

I looked around for Owen. He was at the end of the front row with his family.

A few minutes later, the lights flickered. The show was about to start.

I crossed my fingers. I knew that no matter what, *the show must go on.*

The curtains were closed. One microphone stood in front. Mr. Guidi came out, and everyone clapped. He closed his eyes and did a bunch of little tiny bows.

"Welcome," he said. "Thank you all for coming."

My heart was beating fast. I was probably just as nervous as Nia.

Mr. Guidi said, "We are proud to present to you today our musical, *Willa Wonka and the Chocolate Factory.*"

The audience cheered again, and the photographer kneeled in front of the stage. She took a lot of pictures of Mr. Guidi. Her camera made fast clicking noises. The sound reminded me of the noise Mama's knife made when she was cutting vegetables.

Then I realized something important. The little rips in Nia's coat didn't really look like rips. They looked like *cuts.*

Did someone cut the inside of the coat? I thought. *But why would somebody do that?*

Mr. Guidi was still talking, but I wasn't paying attention. I was thinking about the mystery.

Then the light bulb in my brain turned on.

The coat is just like my circuit kit! I realized. If everything was connected the right way, the light bulb turned on. But if the circuit was interrupted, the light wouldn't work.

Last night, my light bulb hadn't been screwed in all the way. That meant it wouldn't turn on. Once I tightened it, the circuit worked.

What if those holes in Nia's coat are *cuts?* I thought. *And someone made them so they could loosen the bulbs?*

That would explain why the lights didn't work, even though the remote did. And if the circuit was still disconnected, the coat wouldn't work tonight.

Onstage, Mr. Guidi said, "I hope you enjoy the show." Then he disappeared behind the curtain.

I could *not* let the show start. I had to talk to Mr. Guidi right away!

CHAPTER 9

SURPRISES

I popped out of my seat and ran to the stage. "Azaleah!" I heard Mama call. But I kept going. There was no time to waste.

I climbed up the stairs to the side of the stage and scooted behind the curtains. Andrea was there, ready to open them. She looked surprised to see me.

Before she could say anything, I said, "Andrea, please don't open the curtains. I have to talk to Mr. Guidi."

Andrea looked at the curtains, then back at me. "You have two minutes," she said.

I nodded and ran to Mr. Guidi. Two minutes was enough.

"Azaleah, what are you doing back here?" Mr. Guidi asked when he saw me. "I told you that you can't be backstage today."

I was out of breath. "I have to talk to you," I panted. "In private."

"Make it fast," Mr. Guidi said. He looked at the actors. "Everyone, take your places onstage." Then he led me to the side and squatted down. "What is it?"

"I think I know what's wrong with Nia's coat," I whispered. "I think I can fix it."

Mr. Guidi's face lit up. "Are you sure?"

I nodded. "Almost positive."

"Let's go!" Mr. Guidi grabbed my hand.

We ran to the dressing room. Nia was already wearing her costume.

"Nia, give me the coat," I said. "I think I figured it out!"

"Forget it," said Nia. "It's too late."

"Let her try," said Mr. Guidi.

I took the coat and turned it inside out. I examined the holes. They were too straight to be rips. Someone had *definitely* made the cuts on purpose.

I put my finger inside one cut and found a light bulb. I was right—it was loose!

I tightened it and looked up at Nia and Mr. Guidi. They stared at me.

Chris and Mike stood at the dressing room door. Chris turned on his recorder and watched me very closely.

I put my fingers through every hole and checked every light bulb. They were *all* loose. Nia stood next to me while I tightened each light bulb. I could tell she was holding her breath.

Finally I said, "Mike, turn on the coat."

Mike grabbed the remote from a shelf and pushed the button. The coat lit right up. We waited to see if the lights would blink or turn off. They didn't!

Nia hugged me. Mike clapped and smiled. Mr. Guidi yelled, "Bravo, Azaleah! You saved the show."

I grinned at Nia. "Break a leg."

She laughed, and Mr. Guidi grabbed my hand again. "Come, Azaleah! We're running late!"

Mr. Guidi led me back to the stage and around the curtain. The audience had been whispering, but they stopped when they saw us. Mr. Guidi gave me a little bow and helped me jump down.

When I got back to my seat, Auntie Sam looked confused. Mama and Daddy looked a little bit angry.

Mr. Guidi stood at the microphone and straightened his throat. "I apologize for the slight delay," he said. "And now, our gift to you . . . *Willa Wonka and the Chocolate Factory*!"

The crowd cheered again, and the curtains opened. I got comfortable in my seat. This was going to be a good show.

When Nia's imagination song came on, the whole stage got dark except for a small spotlight. The song started out quiet, and Nia's coat lights came on.

The louder Nia sang, the brighter the lights glowed. The coat did exactly what it was supposed to do! It was amazing.

At the end of the show, the cast got a standing ovation. Then the actors came out a few at a time for the curtain call. The audience clapped for all of them. Nia was the last one to come out because she was the star.

When Nia bowed, the crowd went wild! I looked at Owen. He was standing on his seat and cheering. Then he jumped down and grabbed some flowers from under his seat. He ran to the front of the stage and handed them to Nia.

Nia looked shocked. I *was* shocked.

On the way back to his seat, Owen passed me. "Your sister was awesome," he said. "Did you have something to do with the coat working?"

I nodded.

Owen said, "Great job! The coat and Nia's voice were the perfect match. They were beautiful."

I smiled. "Thanks." But I was still confused about one thing. "Owen . . . why were you laughing during the rehearsals?"

Owen blushed and looked down. "I don't know. All that stuff was going wrong," he said. "I guess I thought it was funny."

"It *wasn't* funny," I said.

"I know," said Owen. "I don't know what I would have done if I'd had to deal with all those problems. I feel bad about laughing. That's why I brought flowers."

Owen returned to his seat. He climbed up on his chair and clapped some more.

The audience hollered and clapped for Nia for a long time. She smiled at everyone. Then the actors joined hands and bowed again. Finally the curtains closed.

People started to leave the theater, but our family stayed to wait for Nia. There was still one thing I was not happy about. This mystery wasn't solved. Owen wasn't the culprit . . . and that meant someone else was.

CHAPTER 10

A SHINING STAR
(OR TWO)

It was time for Chris to start his interviews. Nia, the boy who played Charlie, and the boy who played Charlie's grandpa all came back to the stage.

First, they stood together to have their picture taken. Then, Chris interviewed Charlie and his grandpa.

The whole time, I watched everyone very closely. The only people in the room were Mr. Guidi, Chris, the photographer, the actors, and their families.

Since Owen wasn't a suspect anymore, I had to start from scratch. I thought about all the things listed in my notebook. I had written down everything that went wrong:

- broken props and curtain strings
- missing batteries
- messed-up lights
- microphones turning off
- an empty bubble machine

I had also made a list of suspects, but it wasn't any of them.

Finally, it was Nia's turn to be interviewed.

Chris said, "Nia, your performance was phenomenal. Tell us a bit about how you prepare for a show like this."

"Well," said Nia, "I spend a lot of time in my room practicing. I memorize the dance routines and the songs. I try to get so good that I don't have to think as hard to remember my lines."

Chris nodded and wrote something down. The photographer took a picture.

"But," said Nia, "sometimes that's not enough. Sometimes things go wrong, and I can't do anything about it."

Chris frowned. "What do you mean?"

"We had some rough rehearsals for this show. My coat didn't work at the dress rehearsal." Nia smiled at me. "But somehow my sister figured out that the light bulbs needed tightening."

Chris's frown got bigger. "Do you think it was the ghost of Thespis?"

"No," Nia said, shaking her head. "I don't believe in ghosts. I have a feeling a *person* tried to ruin our show."

Chris gasped and covered his mouth. "Who would do such a thing?"

I had seen lots of shows with lots of good actors. Chris was a bad actor. Chris was faking it. He *knew* who did it.

And now I thought I might too. What if *Chris* was the one who had played tricks on everyone? He was allowed to go wherever he wanted in the theater. Mr. Guidi had even said he let Chris explore backstage.

It would have been easy for Chris to loosen props and plugs. He could have emptied the bubble machine. He could have taken the batteries and messed with the curtain strings. Worst of all, he could have ruined Nia's coat.

But why? I wondered.

"I don't know who did it," Nia answered. "I'm just grateful that my sister Azaleah is a good detective. She saved the show."

Nia pointed at me. Mr. Guidi, Mama, Daddy, Auntie Sam, and Tiana smiled at me.

The photographer walked over and took a close-up of me.

"Chris," she said, "come interview Azaleah!"

Chris walked over slowly. He didn't look excited. "Azaleah, how did you know what was wrong with the coat?" he asked.

I couldn't believe they were interviewing me. Maybe I would be in the newspaper too. I told them about my investigation.

". . . then my circuit kit light didn't work last night," I explained. "It turned out the light bulb wasn't screwed all the way in. That helped me realize that someone had loosened the bulbs in the coat."

Chris frowned the whole time I talked. He didn't write down anything.

How is he going to remember what I said? I worried. *He won't be able to write a good story.*

That's when it hit me. *A good story. That's* what Chris was after. He wanted to write about the ghost of Thespis. I was positive. He had mentioned the ghost more than anyone else.

I ran over to Mr. Guidi. His eyes got big when I whispered in his ear.

"Chris, Azaleah thinks you tried to create some drama of your own so you could write a good story. Is that true?" Mr. Guidi crossed his arms.

Chris looked down. We all stared at him, but he didn't answer.

"Chris?" said Mr. Guidi.

"Yes. I did it," Chris admitted. He looked at Nia. "I'm really sorry. I wasn't trying to be mean. I just wanted to write a good story."

Nia's mouth dropped open. "You tried to ruin our show so you could write about it?"

Chris looked sad. "I'm sorry," he said again. "I didn't think about how miserable I might make all of you. I just wanted people to read my article. I thought the ghost of Thespis would make a good story."

"You almost ruined our show," Nia said. "How could you?"

Chris shook his head. "This was the best show I've ever seen," he said. "I'll be writing an excellent review in the paper. I'll tell the truth. I'll apologize to everyone in my article."

The photographer spoke up. "Nia and Azaleah, I'd like a picture of the two of you together."

I hopped onstage, and Nia put her arm around me. I noticed that Mr. Guidi was talking to Chris in a corner of the theater. Chris looked very sad. I knew he was in big trouble.

"Look at me," said the photographer.

Nia and I grinned while the camera made its fast clicking sounds.

Daddy said, "The triple threat and her sister, Detective Azaleah."

* * *

The whole way to Avec Amour, we talked about the musical. Nia was so happy she couldn't stop smiling. When she saw the back room at the restaurant, she really smiled.

My CONGRATULATIONS! sign was hanging on the wall. Mama had set up a dessert table with sweets. It was just like in Willa Wonka's Chocolate Factory. It was the best party ever!

At the end of the party, Daddy took out his laptop. "Let's see if the review is online yet," he said.

We all crowded around to look at the newspaper's website. There was a big picture of me and Nia. Underneath, it said, *Nia the triple threat and her sister, Detective Azaleah.* Next to the picture it said: *Article coming soon! Five Stars for* Willa Wonka and the Chocolate Factory*!*

Nia hugged me and yelled, "We're going to be famous!"

I hugged her back, then went over to the dessert table. I chose some of Mama's delicious treats to take home. I wanted leftovers, just in case another mystery popped up. Good detectives needed a snack!

ABOUT THE
AUTHOR

Nikki Shannon Smith is from Oakland, California, but she now lives in the Central Valley with her husband and two children. She has worked in elementary education for more than twenty-five years, and writes everything from picture books to young adult novels. When she's not busy with family, work, or writing, she loves to visit the coast. The first thing she packs in her suitcase is always a book.

GLOSSARY

assumption (uh-SUHMP-shuhn)—something accepted as true

coincidence (koh-IN-si-duhns)—something that happens accidentally at the same time as something else but seems to have a connection

culprit (KUHL-prit)—a person accused of, charged with, or guilty of a crime or fault

curious (KYOOR-ee-uhs)—eager to explore and learn about new things

evidence (E-vuh-duhnts)—information, items, and facts that help prove something is true or false

foul play (foul pley)—unfair or dishonest acts

intermission (in-ter-MISH-uhn)—a pause or short break (as between acts of a play)

lead (leed)—the main role in a movie or play

motive (MOH-tiv)—a reason for doing something

observant (uhb-ZUR-vuhnt)—quick to take notice

ovation (oh-VEY-shuhn)—an expression of approval or enthusiasm made by clapping or cheering

phenomenal (fi-NOM-uh-nuhl)—very remarkable

rehearsal (ri-HURSS-uhl)—a private performance or practice session in preparation for a public appearance

review (ri-VYOO)—a newspaper or magazine article that gives an opinion on a product such as a book or film

sabotage (SAB-uh-tahzh)—damage or destruction of property that is done on purpose

suspect (SUHSS-pekt)—someone who may be responsible for a crime

understudy (UHN-der-stuhd-ee)—an actor who is prepared to take over another actor's part if necessary

wings (wingz)—an area just off the stage of a theater

LET'S TALK!

1. *The Dramatic Life of Azaleah Lane* is a mystery, and you don't know who the culprit is until the end. Who did you expect to be behind the rehearsal mishaps? What evidence from the book were you using to draw your conclusion? Were you right or wrong? Talk about it with a friend or family member.

2. Imagine you are Mr. Guidi, and Chris has just told you he caused all of the problems. Chris has also apologized. Do you think there should be consequences? Why or why not? What should it be? Discuss it with a partner.

3. There is a lot of talk about the ghost of Thespis throughout this story. Do you think the ghost is real? Why or why not? Share your opinion with a partner, and give some evidence from the story if you can.

4. Who is your favorite character in *The Dramatic Life of Azaleah Lane*? Tell a partner who you like best, and give two reasons why.

LET'S WRITE!

1. At the end of this story, Chris says he will include an apology in his newspaper article. Imagine you are Chris, and write an apology letter to the cast of *Willa Wonka and the Chocolate Factory*.

2. The rehearsals for Nia's show had a lot of flaws. Think about all of the problems that happened. Can you make a list of all of them in order? It's OK to use the book for help!

3. Azaleah and Nia are extra worried about the show going well because there is going to be a review posted online. A review is when someone writes a short description of something and gives his or her opinion about it. Try writing your own review of this book. Start with a few sentences telling what happened. Then write your opinion. Did you enjoy the story? Why or why not?

4. Think about the main character, Azaleah Lane. Do you think you and Azaleah are alike or different? Write a short paragraph describing your differences or similarities.

ACT IT OUT!

The Lane family is full of drama in this story! You can be an actor too. Decide who you'd like to pretend to be. It can be someone from this book, another book, a movie, or a play. It can even be someone you make up. Make a costume, write a script, and then introduce yourself to someone at home.

Follow the steps below to get started! This activity can be done alone or with a friend or sibling.

Make a Costume!

1. First, ask for permission to use your clothes, or old clothes and costumes you have at home. You might also need permission to use materials for a paper costume.

2. Decide who you are going to be. A person? An animal? A character you've heard of? Someone or something you've imagined? If you're stuck, you can wear your real clothes and pretend you're Detective Azaleah!

3. If your character doesn't already have a name, choose one.

4. Now look around at home for things you can use to make a costume. Here are some ideas:
   - old or borrowed clothes or old Halloween costumes
   - hats
   - sunglasses
   - scarves
   - gloves
   - coats
   - shoes
   - sheets, blankets, or towels

*You can even make things out of paper, tape, staples, glue, crayons, and scissors!

5. Try on your costume and make sure it's not going to have any problems, like Nia's did in the story! Is your costume ready? Now you need a script! (A script is a paper with the words you are supposed to say written on it.)

Write a Script!

You will need a piece of paper and a pen or pencil. Don't forget your imagination!

1. Get into character. You will have to introduce yourself. Write down what you will say. Here are some ideas to help your audience get to know your character:
   - What is your name?
   - How old are you?
   - Where are you from?
   - What are some interesting details about you?
   - What problem do you need to tell your audience about?
   - What do you want to explain to your audience?

2. Practice reading your script at least three times. If you want, you can practice until you have it memorized like Nia!

3. Find someone at home and ask when they are available to watch your performance. Then act out your script while you wear your costume. Don't forget to take a bow!